WINNERS TAKE ALL

For Julia —

Readers are winners.

All-Star Sports Story series

WINNERS TAKE ALL

FRED BOWEN

PEACHTREE
ATLANTA

Published by
PEACHTREE PUBLISHERS
1700 Chattahoochee Avenue
Atlanta, Georgia 30318-2112

www.peachtree-online.com

Major League Baseball trademarks and copyrights are used with permission
of Major League Baseball Properties, Inc.

Photo of Christy Mathewson courtesy of the National Baseball Hall of Fame
Library, Cooperstown, NY.

Cover design by Thomas Gonzalez and Maureen Withee
Book design by Melanie McMahon Ives and Loraine M. Joyner

Printed in January 2014 in the United States of America by R.R. Donnelley
and Sons, Harrisonburg, Virginia
10 9 8 7 6 5 4
Revised Edition

Library of Congress Cataloging-in-Publication Data

Bowen, Fred.
  Winners take all / written by Fred Bowen.
      p. cm.
  Summary: When Kyle fakes a catch, his baseball team goes on to win the
league championship but Kyle doesn't feel good about winning by cheating.
Includes a section on the sportsmanship of Christy Mathewson, a pitcher who
played professional baseball in the early 1900s.
  ISBN 978-1-56145-512-6
  [1. Baseball--Fiction. 2. Honesty--Fiction. 3. Sportsmanship--Fiction.] I. Title.
  PZ7.B6724Wi 2009
  [Fic]--dc22
                                    2009017029

To the memory of a great friend,
Sam Katz (1951–1980)

ONE

"Rally caps!" Kyle Holt shouted as he marched down the Reds bench. All at once, his teammates turned their caps around. They were pumped. It was the top of the sixth, the last inning of the game. The Reds were down 3–2 against the Cubs, their archrivals. It was definitely time for rally caps.

Kyle was too nervous to sit down. He leaned forward against the tall chain-link fence in front of the Reds bench, his hands clutching a couple of high links. Nate Bloom and Claire Jenkins, his teammates and best friends, were pressed against it too.

"Down by a run," Nate said, shaking his head. "We gotta come back."

"Yeah," Claire agreed. "Or we'll be one game behind the Cubs in the standings with only two games left to play."

"Yeah, and if the Cubs win, they'll never let us forget it," Kyle said.

The Reds and the Cubs were the top teams in the eleven- and twelve-year-olds' Rising Stars League. And they were locked in a tight battle for first place—with only ten days left in the season.

The bleachers were packed with parents, brothers, sisters, friends, and neighbors—practically half the town. Nobody wanted to miss this game.

Kyle looked out onto the field past second base to the wooden fence lining the outfield and to the thick woods behind it. This was his favorite place in the world—especially when the Reds were playing the Cubs.

Alana Garvey, the Reds leadoff batter this inning, came up to bat.

"Come on, Alana," Kyle called out.

"You go, girl!" Claire yelled.

The first pitch came in a little high. Alana chased it and popped up to the shortstop.

One out.

Kyle, Nate, and Claire watched silently as Alana trudged off the field. Dylan Reffe was up next. Claire crossed her fingers against the fence.

"Come on, Dylan!" Nate shouted. "Start us off."

Dylan smacked the ball into center field and raced to first base. Kyle, Nate, and Claire went wild, cheering and pounding the fence. Everyone on the Reds bench jumped to their feet and started pounding the fence too.

Coach Daye's voice quickly cut through the cheers: "Salvador, you're up. Kyle's on deck. Nate's in the hole."

Kyle grabbed a bat and took some practice swings as Salvador Rodriguez struck out on three blazing fastballs.

"Two outs!" Bryan Ford, the Cubs catcher, shouted as he held up two fingers.

Kyle took his stance, spreading his feet out in the batter's box and tapping the plate with his bat.

"Well, well, look who's gonna make the

last out," Bryan taunted Kyle from under his mask.

Kyle tried to ignore Bryan, like he always did.

The first pitch streaked across the outside corner.

Strike one!

"No batter!" Bryan yelled as he tossed the ball back. "What's the matter, Kyle?" he sneered. "Too fast for you?"

Kyle stepped out of the batter's box and glanced at Bryan. *I'd like to punch that guy*, he thought.

"Just meet it. Only takes one!" someone shouted from the stands. Kyle knew the voice right away. It was his dad's. His dad came to all the games and always cheered the loudest.

"Swing level!" his father yelled.

Kyle choked up on his bat and stepped back into the box. His eyes narrowed as the second pitch spun toward him.

Crack!

Kyle banged a grounder clear into left field. Dylan cruised into second and Kyle reached first with time to spare.

The Reds were coming back!

Now it was up to Nate to keep the rally alive.

"Two outs. Run on anything!" Coach Daye shouted to Kyle and Dylan.

Nate crushed a line drive into the gap between two outfielders, and Dylan and Kyle took off. Dylan easily made it home to tie the game as Kyle was powering toward third. Kyle saw the third-base coach wildly windmilling his arm and turned on the jets.

He sprinted across home plate with the crowd's cheers ringing in his ears.

The Reds had pushed ahead! The score was 4–3.

One out later, Kyle hustled out to his position in center field for the bottom of the final inning. "Come on, Reds!" he shouted as he ran. "Just need three outs."

The first two Cubs batters popped up to the infield and the Reds moved two outs closer to the win.

"One more out," Kyle pleaded as he pounded his glove and paced in center field.

The next Cubs batter stepped up to the

plate and settled into his stance. The first pitch was low, but the batter looped a single to left field. Now the Cubs had a runner on first with two outs, and Bryan Ford was coming to the plate.

"No batter!" Kyle yelled, but he didn't believe it. *Bryan may be a jerk, but he is a slugger,* Kyle thought. "Move back," Kyle called to Claire in left field, waving her back with his hand.

The first two pitches missed their mark. "Throw strikes!" Kyle shouted, sensing trouble. He didn't want to lose this game. Not in front of all these people. Not in front of his dad.

The next pitch cut the heart of the plate. Bryan swung hard and sent the ball soaring deep into left center field. Kyle raced after it, barreling to the edge of the field.

The outfield fence came up fast, but Kyle couldn't slow down. He pushed his right foot down in front of it and leaped as high as he could. His right hand found the top of the fence and pushed him even higher. He twisted his head back and saw the ball falling toward him. He stretched his glove out to grab it.

The Reds hopes for first place were riding with the ball.

I've got to get it! Kyle thought.

Two

Thwack! The ball rocketed into the webbing of Kyle's outstretched glove just as his thigh collided with the top of the wooden fence. The force of the ball and the momentum of his leap sent Kyle cartwheeling over the fence—first his glove, then his arms, head, and legs. He landed on his back on the dirt strip between the fence and the woods.

He wasted no time worrying about pain and instantly twisted his head left to check his glove. *The ball!* he thought. The ball—and the game—had slipped out of his glove and lay just inches away.

Suddenly, Kyle's mind was a jumble of thoughts. *If they think I didn't make the catch, we lose the game...Bryan will brag his head off...Why did he hit the home run?...But it wasn't a home run...I made the catch...No one can see through the fence...We deserve to win...We're better than the Cubs....*

Kyle reached over and snapped up the ball with his glove. He popped to his feet, spun toward the field, and held the ball— now tight in his glove—high above the fence for everyone to see.

The scene on the field washed over Kyle like a wave. The Reds fans were cheering like crazy and the Cubs fans were groaning out loud. The infield ump, running to the fence, stopped midstep, thrust his thumb in the air, and shouted, "Out!"

Bryan Ford slowed to a trot as he rounded second base and then kicked the dirt. Claire was jumping up and down and screaming, "What a catch! What a catch!"

Kyle picked his cap off the ground and swung himself over the fence. The Reds fans raced to the outfield, whooping and leaping in celebration.

They were not alone.

Mr. Rolfe, the Cubs coach, now red faced and waving his arms, ran onto the field too. "That's a home run!" he yelled. "He didn't catch the ball *in the field!*"

The two coaches and the two umpires huddled in the outfield. Mr. Rolfe was still shouting and pointing toward the fence. Coach Daye stood quietly with his arms folded.

One of the umpires reached into his pocket for a rule book and began leafing through it. The other ump took off his cap and scratched his head.

Meanwhile, Kyle's teammates were mobbing him and shouting out.

"Circus catch!"

"Did you see that grab?"

"Somebody call SportsCenter!"

Kyle got bounced around but he kept a tight grip on the ball. Everything was happening so fast. The outfield was quickly filling with the two teams, their parents, and fans. Everyone was yelling at once. Kyle stepped away from his celebrating teammates to hear what the parents were saying.

"He was over the fence!"

"So what? He caught the ball in front of it."

"Well, he didn't stay in the field of play!"

"That doesn't matter!"

"How do you know he really caught it?"

"He held up the ball. You saw him!"

Then a Reds mom and a Cubs dad went nose to nose.

"The ump said it was an out!" insisted the mom, stabbing the air with an angry finger.

"The ump couldn't see anything. He was way out of position," the dad snapped, pushing his face into the mom's.

"He was in a much better position than you were!" the mom shouted right back.

"That kid didn't catch the ball in the field and you know it!" The dad's eyes were blazing and his face was flushed.

Kyle felt like he was in the middle of a bad dream. He inched back a couple of steps. He wanted to go home. Fast.

Kyle spotted his dad across the field, still cheering and clapping. He felt sick. He wished he could put his life on rewind and start the game all over again. But there was no going back now.

Part of him wanted to admit right then and there that he had faked the catch. But he just couldn't. What would everybody think of him?

Then he heard Nate shouting to all the others in the crowd, "It doesn't matter what we say! It's what the umps say."

That's right! Kyle thought. *Yeah, it's what the umps say that counts. They make the calls. That's their job. My job is to play to win.*

The crowd began to press closer to the umpires.

"Whoa! Everybody get back," the home-plate umpire ordered. "Coaches too."

"He wasn't on the field of play! The catch doesn't count!" Mr. Rolfe screamed again.

"What do you know?" Mr. Daye shot back. "You're not the umpire."

"Coaches, you are both way out of line!"

the ump shouted. "Everybody step back!"

Mr. Rolfe took two stingy steps back, but Mr. Daye didn't budge. Everyone else shuffled back as the chatter settled into low grumbling. The two umpires walked several steps to the edge of the infield grass. They spoke together in low voices. Then the home-plate umpire nodded, turned, and walked toward the crowd. Suddenly, everyone was quiet.

The home-plate umpire opened his mouth to announce the decision.

Kyle wasn't sure what he wanted the ump to say.

He squeezed the ball with his glove so hard that his hand ached.

THREE

The batter is out!" the umpire declared. "The catch is good." The Reds players and parents burst into cheers again. The umpire walked away from the crowd with Mr. Rolfe trailing behind, shaking his fist and arguing the call.

Kyle just looked down at the ball in his glove. The Reds gathered around him and tried to lift him up on their shoulders, but Kyle twisted free and managed to stay firmly on the ground. His teammates started slapping high fives. Kyle slapped a few hands too, but not very hard.

Coach Daye wrapped his arm around Kyle's shoulder with a hearty squeeze. "You saved the day, Kyle!" he shouted loud enough for all the Reds to hear. "Put the Reds right in first place!"

The Reds coach lowered his voice as he watched the Cubs quietly leaving the field. "And you almost gave Coach Rolfe a heart attack." He flashed a sly smile and added, "I love beating Coach Rolfe. His Cubs have been beating my Reds for years."

"Um, yeah, Coach," Kyle said as he scanned the crowd again for his parents. He really wanted to go home. Suddenly he saw his dad waving like crazy.

"Over here, champ!" his dad called.

"Gotta go, Coach," Kyle said as he scooted out from under Coach Daye's arm.

But there was no getting away from the victory celebration. On the car ride home, his parents—especially his dad—couldn't talk about anything but Kyle's now-famous catch.

"Unbelievable!" his dad crowed, shaking his head and smiling proudly. "What an unbelievable catch!"

Unbelievable, Kyle thought as he squirmed in the backseat.

Kyle's mother turned around and smiled warmly at Kyle. "It was a great catch," she said. "I can't wait to tell Honsey."

Honsey was Kyle's eighty-year-old baseball-loving grandmother who lived with Kyle's family. Honsey might forget where she left her glasses or mix up the names of Kyle's friends, but she could tell you the winners of every World Series all the way back to 1903.

Luckily, the car ride wasn't too long. The Holts lived near the baseball field in an old neighborhood crowded with houses and kids. Kyle lived two doors down from Claire, in a brick house just like hers. They had been friends since they met in the sandbox at the neighborhood park.

"Honsey! Erin! We're home!" Mr. Holt called as they walked through the front door.

Kyle's fifteen-year-old sister Erin emerged from the den. Honsey trailed behind, moving gently with her cane.

"How did the Reds do?" Honsey asked.

"They won, 4–3," Kyle's father announced,

putting his arm around Kyle and pulling him close. "And your grandson made an unbelievable catch to save the game. Tell her, Kyle."

"Uh, I just got lucky. The whole team played great," said Kyle, trying to smile really big.

"Lucky?" his father repeated in a booming voice. "Honsey, this boy ran back, jumped up, fell over the fence, and still hung on to the ball."

Honsey's eyes widened as Mr. Holt acted out Kyle's catch across the living room.

"It was the best catch I have ever seen!" Kyle's father said as he fell onto the couch, popped up, and held a pretend baseball high in the air.

"I'm surprised you didn't break your neck falling over that fence," Kyle's mom added, shaking her head.

"This boy sounds like another Willie Mays." Honsey smiled proudly.

"How do you mean?" asked Kyle.

"Greatest catch I ever saw was Willie Mays's over-the-shoulder catch in the first game of the 1954 World Series between the New York Giants and the Cleveland Indians," Honsey said.

Yeah, but Willie Mays probably held onto the ball, Kyle thought.

Honsey continued her story. "Vic Wertz of the Indians must have hit the ball 500 feet to dead center field in the old Polo Grounds in New York. Mays still ran back and got it." Honsey pointed to her daughter, Kyle's mom. "You were at the game with your father and me. You just didn't know it. You were born three months later."

Kyle's mother just smiled and nodded. She had heard the story a thousand times before.

"Well, even Willie Mays didn't go over the fence to get the ball like Kyle did," Mr. Holt pointed out.

"If he'd had to, he would have," Honsey said flatly. Then she looked at Kyle and said in her matter-of-fact way, "It sounds like you've got the makings of a real ballplayer."

"Thanks, Honsey," Kyle said.

The doorbell rang. It was Claire. She was

still in uniform and still smiling. "Hey, Kyle," she said, waving a twenty-dollar bill. "My mom and dad said they would treat us to sundaes at York Ice Cream."

"Uh, sure," Kyle said.

"Sounds like a great idea," his mother chimed in.

"Does this mean you guys have already won the championship?" Erin asked.

"Not yet. But we're in first place," Claire said. "We're one game ahead of the Cubs, but we still have two games left to play."

"Hey, Kyle," his dad said. "We've got to put today's win on the refrigerator." Kyle and Mr. Holt always recorded the Reds wins and losses on the team schedule posted on the refrigerator behind a big pizzeria magnet.

Before Kyle could say anything, his father was off to the kitchen and marking down the score. "Hey, it looks like you've got another game with the Cubs," his father called.

"Yeah, I know," Kyle called back.

"It's a makeup game. The first one got rained out," Claire said.

Just as Mr. Holt came back into the room, the phone rang. Erin raced past him to answer it and returned quickly. "Kyle, it's for you," she said. "I don't recognize the voice."

"It's probably the newspapers wanting to interview the hero of the game," Claire teased.

"Or some pro scout who heard about your catch," his father said.

"Cut it out," Kyle said good-naturedly. "The whole team won that game." Then he walked into the den.

"Hello?" Kyle said into the phone.

The voice on the other end got straight to the point: "I know you didn't make that catch."

FOUR

Who is this?" Kyle demanded. He kept his voice low so the others in the living room couldn't hear.

"It doesn't matter who I am," said the voice. "But I saw you go over the fence today and I know you didn't make the catch."

Kyle's heart pounded. A bitter taste welled up in the back of his throat. "What do you mean? Who is this?" Kyle said, trying to sound tough instead of scared.

"I know you didn't make that catch," the voice repeated.

"What do you want from me?" Kyle was starting to panic, but he kept his voice just above a whisper.

"Why don't we talk about this tomorrow?"

"Who are you?"

"Meet me at the field, right where you made the catch. Or should I say, where you *didn't* make the catch," the voice replied.

"Come on, Kyle," Claire called from the living room. "Let's go. My stomach is grumbling for some ice cream."

Kyle covered the mouthpiece of the phone with his hand. "All right," he called back.

"Listen, I gotta go," Kyle whispered into the phone.

The voice spit out the instructions. "Tomorrow morning. Nine o'clock. At the field. Between the outfield fence and the woods."

"Okay," Kyle said. He hung up the phone and stared blankly at the floor.

Just then, Claire came into the den. "Come on," she insisted, pulling Kyle toward the door. "Ice cream. Remember?"

"Oh, yeah," Kyle said.

The two of them made their way into the living room, but Kyle couldn't shake off the phone call. He was still thinking about the voice on the phone and the mess he was in.

"Who was that on the phone?" his mother asked.

Kyle jerked his head back, startled. "Oh," Kyle said, "just some kid calling about the game."

"You're famous now, Kyle," his father said proudly. "Believe me, anyone who saw that catch just won't be able to stop talking about it. I know I can't."

That's for sure! Kyle thought.

"Are you okay, Kyle?" his mother asked.

"Yeah, I'm just tired. And my leg hurts a little bit. I'll be all right." He forced a smile and his mother smiled back.

"Well," she said, "you two go ahead. Enjoy your ice cream."

Kyle barely said a word as he walked with Claire up the street past children play-ing in their yards. York Ice Cream was just two blocks away.

Claire stopped at the corner to let a car go by and glanced at Kyle. "You don't seem much like a guy who made the greatest catch in the history of the Rising Stars League," she said.

Kyle couldn't bear to look at his friend, so he gazed up and down the street, half-heartedly checking for cars. *I've known Claire my whole life,* he thought. *I've got to tell her something....*

"You know that call I got?" Kyle said finally as they started to cross the street.

"Yeah?" Claire said.

"It was some guy who says I didn't make the catch to win the game," Kyle said.

Claire stopped abruptly as they reached the other side of the street. "What are you talking about?"

Kyle repeated what the caller had said, word for word.

"He's crazy," Claire said, her face twisting into a scowl.

"Yeah, but—"

"Who cares what he thinks? The game is over," Claire said as she started walking again.

"It sounds like he wants to make trouble," Kyle said, matching Claire's stride.

"What kind of trouble?"

Kyle shrugged. "I don't know. But he wants me to meet him down at the field tomorrow morning."

"Why?"

"I don't know."

"You going?" Claire asked as they neared York Ice Cream. Several kids were eating at the outside tables.

"I don't know," Kyle said, shaking his head. "Maybe I should."

Claire stopped short so they could finish their conversation before heading inside. "Maybe the whole team should go," she said.

Kyle shook his head firmly. "I don't want everybody to know about this," he said.

Claire didn't say anything at first. Then she said, "I think you've got to go see this guy. If you don't go, he'll think you really didn't make the catch."

Kyle nodded. He didn't want to have to tell Claire the truth. And maybe he wouldn't have to. Maybe the caller didn't really see anything. Nobody could have seen through the fence.

"What time?" Claire asked.

"What?"

"What time are you supposed to meet him?"

"Nine o'clock. Why?"

"Because I'm gonna go with you," she said. "We're gonna figure out what this guy's up to."

FIVE

When Claire and Kyle arrived at the outfield fence, a brisk wind was kicking up loose dirt and spinning it in tiny pools. Kyle stared at the narrow dirt strip. He could almost see the baseball lying there again, just inches from his glove.

Claire watched the steel-gray clouds. "It looks like it's going to rain buckets," she said. "This guy had better show up soon."

"It's 8:57," Kyle said, checking his watch.

The treetops danced as the wind picked up. *We're going to get soaked*, Kyle thought.

Claire looked around. "Why did he want to meet here?"

"I don't know, it's nothing but woods and dirt," Kyle said.

"Did you see anybody back here when you made the catch?"

"No," Kyle said, shaking his head. "Did you see anybody? I mean, could you see over the top of the fence from left field?"

"No, I didn't see anybody."

A chill swept over Kyle. He looked at the darkening clouds. They looked like they were about to burst.

"What time is it?" Claire asked.

"9:02," said Kyle.

Crackle.

A sharp noise came from the edge of the trees. Kyle and Claire spun toward the woods as a teenager stepped out. His hair was short and he was wearing a loose sweatshirt and baggy jeans with a chain swooping down from his belt loop to his back pocket.

Kyle leaned toward Claire and whispered, "I know him!"

Claire nodded. "Yeah, he's Jason Ridauer. He played for Mr. Rolfe and the Cubs a couple of years ago. He's trouble."

Kyle moved cautiously toward Jason. Claire stayed behind. "You called me," Kyle said, sounding a lot more confident than he felt.

"Yeah, that was me." Jason's voice was flat, like he was too cool or too bored to talk.

"So what do you want?" Kyle asked with a quick glance up to the brooding clouds. "We don't have much time."

"I don't need much time," Jason said with a crooked little smile. "I just want you to know that I'm serious."

"Serious about what?" Kyle replied.

"Serious about telling the whole league that you're a cheater," Jason said. "You stole that game from the Cubs and it better not cost them the championship."

Claire stepped toward Jason. "What do you know about anything?" she said.

"I was standing right here. I was taking a shortcut through the woods. I could see the whole thing," Jason said. Then he looked at Kyle. "You were lying on the ground and the ball was lying right next to you. Would you like more details?"

Kyle swallowed hard. "The umpire said I made the catch," he insisted.

"The ump couldn't see through a wood fence," Jason said.

The dark clouds started to spit rain. "Why didn't you say something at the game?" Claire demanded.

Jason didn't answer. He wiped some raindrops off his face and locked his eyes on Kyle.

Kyle stared back at Jason. "Because it would have just been his word against mine," Kyle said to Claire without taking his eyes off Jason.

"Let me tell you something, Kyle Holt," Jason said. "The Cubs better win the championship trophy, or your secret won't be a secret anymore. Understand?"

The rain was coming down fast and bouncing off the hard dirt.

"Let's get out of here," Claire said, yanking Kyle's arm. "You know you caught it. Who cares what he says?"

"Yeah, go ahead," Jason sneered. "You know you caught it, don't you?"

Kyle stood in the pelting rain and glared at Jason. Claire started hurrying away, ducking her head to keep the rain off her face. "Come on!" she shouted back, still keeping her head low. "If we win the last two games, none of this matters."

"Remember, Kyle," Jason said, "the Cubs better win the championship, or I'll tell everybody your secret."

"I gotta go," Kyle snapped. He hurried after Claire with the rain slapping against him.

"You're a cheater, Kyle Holt!" Jason yelled after him.

Jason's words chased Kyle out of the park.

Six

Two days later the Reds were locked in a tight game with the Giants. Claire was batting. The Reds were down by one run—it was 6–5 in the bottom of the fourth inning.

But Kyle was still thinking about Jason Ridauer. *I am not a cheater. I made a mistake, that's all,* Kyle told himself.

Suddenly his teammates exploded in wild cheers. Claire had sent a sharp single to center.

Oh, no, Kyle thought as he sized up the game. *If we win, Jason will tell everybody I'm a cheater. I've got to make sure we lose this game. It will be like giving something back after I stole it. It would make everything even,* Kyle assured himself.

"Rally caps!" Nate shouted as he marched down the Reds bench.

Kyle slowly turned his cap around, but he wasn't thinking about the rally. *I've made sure the Reds won lots of ball games,* he told himself. *What's so bad about making sure that we lose this one?*

Max Singh popped up to the Giants first baseman.

Kyle bit back a smile.

One out. Runner on first.

"Nate, you're up. Alana, you're on deck," Coach Daye called out. "Kyle's in the hole. Come on. We need some more hits. Let's start hitting like we're a first-place team, not a bunch of losers."

Kyle put on a helmet and reached into the tangle of bats crisscrossed in the corner of the Reds dugout. He picked out his favorite, a thirty-inch Ken Griffey Jr. model.

Nate struck out on three fastballs. Alana moved into the batter's box and Kyle moved to the on-deck circle. Two outs, runner on first.

Kyle rubbed the handle of his bat and glanced up into the stands. The place where his father usually sat was empty. His dad was on a business trip.

"You'll have to beat the Giants without me," his father had said earlier that morning as he stepped out the door, suitcase in hand. Kyle was glad his father was not at the game. It made trying to lose easier.

"Come on, Alana," Coach Daye called. "Be a hitter."

Kyle glanced at Coach Daye, who was clapping from the edge of the Reds dugout. Kyle knew this game was important to Coach Daye, but it wasn't like the Reds were playing in the World Series.

And Kyle didn't want Jason telling everybody he was cheater!

A crack of the bat startled Kyle. Alana had smacked a hard liner into the gap in left center field.

The Giants center fielder hustled over and fired the ball back into the infield. Claire raced around second and held up at third. Alana slid into second with a double.

Runners on second and third. Two outs.

Kyle stepped into the batter's box. He

knew the pressure was on for him to get a hit, but he was feeling a different kind of pressure. *Striking out should be easy*, he told himself as he took a few weak practice swings.

Kyle watched the first pitch streak by.

"Strike one!" the umpire shouted.

The next pitch was in the dirt.

One ball, one strike.

I can't let every pitch go by, Kyle thought as the Giants pitcher went into his windup. He was almost surprised when his weak swing tipped the pitch into the backstop. *Oh, no. I almost hit that one!*

The next pitch spun in low and outside, but Kyle swung hard, missing it by a foot.

Strike three!

Kyle's teammates encouraged him as he grabbed his glove. "Don't worry," Claire said. "You'll get him next time."

"Yeah," Nate agreed. "We've still got two innings to come back. We're only down by one run."

Then Kyle heard someone in the stands yell: "Strike three! Thank *you*, Kyle Holt!"

It was Bryan Ford. He was sitting with some other Cubs. They were laughing and trading high fives. "What a whiffer! How 'bout an error too?"

Kyle ran out to his position with the Cubs laughter echoing in his ears. *What a bunch of jerks,* he thought as he paced angrily around the outfield. *I didn't know* they *were here.*

The first two batters for the Giants struck out. But then the Giants loaded up the bases with two walks and a clean hit.

Bryan and his buddies started chanting, "Let's go, Giants! Let's go, Giants."

Kyle was still thinking and pacing in center field. *I don't want to lose with Bryan watching!*

Tom Kelly, the Reds pitcher, threw a smoking fastball to the outside corner of the plate. The Giants batter, Asa Nuneo, swung hard and fouled the ball back.

I'm going to start playing like a Reds player! Kyle told himself as Bryan's chant echoed in his ears.

Asa swung at the next pitch and connected. Fooled at first by Asa's big swing,

Kyle took a step back, but then he had to race forward for a chance at the quickly falling pop fly. He almost stumbled as he stretched out his glove and lunged for the ball.

SEVEN

The ball fell deep into the pocket of Kyle's glove as his body hit the ground. He snapped the glove shut and desperately held on, skidding and bumping to a stop along the outfield grass.

The Reds held their breath and then burst into cheers as Kyle struggled to his knees and held the ball above his head.

"All right! What a catch!"

"Call SportsCenter! Again!"

"Grady Sizemore, move over!"

Claire and the rest of the Reds pounded Kyle's back as the team tumbled into the dugout.

Coach Daye shouted over all the cheers, "Great catch, Kyle! Now let's get some runs!" He held up the team score book. "Salvador leads off. Dylan is on deck. Let's get some base runners."

Nate beamed as he plopped down next to Kyle on the long wooden bench. "He's back!" Nate declared. "My man Kyle is back."

But Kyle heard other voices too.

"Are you sure you made *that* catch?" Bryan Ford called from the stands as the other Cubs laughed.

Kyle twisted around toward the stands, his face hot and his eyes blazing.

"Don't worry about them, they're just jealous," Claire said, tugging at Kyle's shirtsleeve. "Let's beat the Giants."

"Yeah," Nate agreed. "We'll take care of the Cubs later."

Kyle turned back toward the baseball diamond, but he had a hard time concentrating. *What did Bryan mean by that crack: Are you sure you made that catch? Has Jason Ridauer already been talking to the Cubs?*

He fidgeted on the bench. *No one's going to believe a creep like Jason over me,* he finally decided.

Kyle's catch at the top of the inning

seemed to spark the Reds. Salvador led with a single to left. Then Dylan put down a nice bunt. The pitcher's throw to first base beat Dylan by a step, but Salvador advanced to second base.

One out. Tying run on second. The team was fired up.

"Rally time."

"Just need a single."

"Come on, keep it going."

Adam Szwed, the Reds next batter, cracked a high hopper over the pitcher's head. The ball bounced toward center field, but Casseia Todd, the Giants shortstop, made a sensational leap and knocked the ball down. Salvador skidded to a stop at third as Adam ran to first. The Reds had runners at the corners, one out.

Tony Skladany, the Reds right fielder, popped up to first base for the second out. Nate smacked the bench with his hand. "Man," he whispered to Kyle, shaking his head. "We needed Tony to get a hit."

"Claire will help us out. You watch," Kyle said.

Claire swung and missed the first two pitches, but then sliced a sinking single to right. Salvador scampered across home plate with the tie run.

Max struck out to end the Reds rally. The score was knotted at 6–6. Kyle and his teammates ran out to the field for the last inning with new hope.

"Come on, Reds!" Kyle yelled from center field. "Good defense. Let's make it a one-two-three inning!"

Sure enough, Tom Kelly, the Reds pitcher, set the Giants down in order. After two strikeouts and a nice running catch by Claire in left, the Reds were back up.

"Top of the order!" Coach Daye shouted. "Nate, Alana, and Kyle. Let's get some base runners."

Nate got the Reds off to a fast start. He smacked a fastball past the diving second baseman and raced to first. The Reds bench was on its feet as Alana moved up to the plate and Kyle walked to the on-deck circle.

"Way to go, Nate."

"Way to start us off."

But not everyone was rooting for the Reds.

Bryan Ford and the rest of the Cubs heckled Kyle as he took his practice swings.

"Come on, Kyle. We need another strikeout."

"No batter, Kyle. No batter."

Alana went down swinging, and Kyle stepped to the plate. He could feel his jaw clench. *No way I'm striking out this time,* he told himself as he pounded the plate with his bat and stared at the Giants pitcher. *What do I care about Jason Ridauer and his dumb threats?*

Kyle kept the Reds rally going by cracking a line drive single to right. Nate poured on the speed. He tore around second and slid feet-first into third.

The Reds had runners on the corners again with one out. The runners stayed put as Salvador popped up to shortstop. The Reds were down to their last out.

"Come on, Dylan." Kyle clapped from first base. "Just meet it."

After watching a strike streak by, Dylan

slipped a hard grounder between first and second. Kyle was off at the crack of the bat. The ball shot low across his path, but Kyle didn't slow down. He jumped right over it and kept speeding toward second.

Nate raced across the plate. The Reds had come from behind to win 7–6! They were still in first place! Everyone bounced in a happy circle near home plate, slapping high fives and chanting, "We're number one. We're number one."

Standing in the middle of the celebration, Kyle's heart suddenly sank. There, just beyond the field, was Bryan Ford. His arms were folded tight, his jaw was set, and his eyes were bearing down on Kyle.

Right next to him stood Jason Ridauer.

EIGHT

The Reds had a few days off before their final game of the season—the final matchup between the Cubs and the Reds. Kyle decided to try to take a few days off from thinking about the championship, Jason, and the mess he was in.

It was a perfect sunbright Saturday afternoon, and Kyle was enjoying a bike ride with Nate and Claire. The sky was clear blue and an easy wind swept across Kyle's face.

The three friends skidded to a stop at the edge of Woodlin Park. Nate pointed to a distant basketball court where four players darted around a single metal basket.

"Hey, let's go play some hoops," Nate said.

Claire glanced at her watch and shook her head. "I better start heading home," she said. "And anyway, basketball is not my game."

Kyle squinted into the distance and tried to make out who the players were. "I'm game," Kyle said.

Claire pedaled away. Kyle and Nate pedaled across the field to the basketball court. Halfway there, Kyle squeezed on his brakes and his bike jerked to a stop. Nate stopped his bike a few yards past Kyle. "What gives?" Nate called back.

Kyle stared at the basketball court. "That's Bryan Ford and some of the other Cubs," he said.

"So what?"

"He's a jerk."

Nate looked at the court. He smiled and arched his eyebrows. "That'll make it more fun to beat him," he said.

Kyle stood with one foot on the ground and the other on the bike pedal. "I don't know."

"You afraid of Bryan?"

"No," Kyle said quickly. "Let's go." He hopped on his bike and started pedaling ahead. Nate hopped on his and pedaled after Kyle.

When the two boys reached the court, they dropped their bikes onto the worn grass.

"Hey," Nate called, unstrapping his helmet. "Can we play?"

Bryan Ford stood near the foul line with the basketball on his hip. He looked Kyle and Nate up and down. "Sure," he said. "We can always use a couple more victims. Just let us finish off these guys. We've only got to get one more basket."

Just then Bryan turned, flicked a pass to Reed Johnson, and broke for the basket. Reed hit Bryan with a quick pass. Bryan spun toward the hoop and nudged a layup off the metal backboard and through the net.

"Boy, Bryan looks like trouble," Nate whispered to Kyle.

"Yeah," Kyle agreed. "I don't know who's going to cover him."

Bryan walked toward Kyle and Nate and smiled confidently. "That's game. Now let's pick new teams."

Kyle looked around the circle of six boys. "Let's shoot for teams," he suggested.

Bryan looked around too. "How about me, Reed, and Derrick against you, Nate, and Gus." Bryan smiled his widest smile yet. "You know, the Cubs against the Reds."

"Gus isn't on the Reds," Kyle pointed out.

"Close enough. Derrick isn't on the Cubs."

"Okay, we'll play with those teams," Nate said, taking up the challenge.

"Who's going to cover Bryan?" Kyle whispered to Nate.

"Why don't you try covering him?"

"Thanks for nothing." Kyle smiled. "Hey, what's the game to?" he called to Bryan.

Bryan answered with a series of clipped instructions. "Game to eleven. Every basket counts one point. Got to win by two baskets. Clear every change of possession past the foul line. Winners out."

Kyle swished a short jumper. "Who calls fouls?" he asked.

"Offense call fouls," Bryan said.

"Man, Bryan talks like he owns the park," Kyle whispered as Nate walked by.

"Maybe we can shut him up," Nate said.

But Bryan kept talking as he scored three quick baskets and put the Cubs in the lead. "You better find someone who can cover me, Nate," he teased after making another basket.

Bryan's big mouth fired up the Reds. A couple of quick jumpers by Nate and a twisting layup by Gus cut the lead to one basket. Kyle drove to the hoop, looking for the tying basket. Bryan slapped at the ball, sending it out of bounds.

"Our ball," Kyle said, following the ball to the grass.

"Come on. It went off your leg," Bryan insisted, pointing at Kyle.

"I never touched it," Kyle said.

Bryan rolled his eyes. "All right," he said finally. "Your ball."

Kyle nailed a long shot to even up the

score, 4–4. The two teams traded baskets and the lead until the score was tied again at 9–9.

Every point was a battle. Kyle's legs ached and he struggled to catch his breath.

"Let's get a good shot!" Nate shouted as Gus ripped down a rebound for the Reds.

A series of quick passes found Kyle open in the corner. Kyle went up for a quick jumper, but Bryan lunged for the block and grazed Kyle's shooting hand.

"Foul," Kyle called as the ball bounced off the rim.

"Foul?" Bryan screamed. "I never touched you!"

Kyle calmly tapped his right wrist. "You got me right here," he said.

Bryan exploded. "That's a wimp call. I never touched you and you know it."

"Offense call fouls," Nate reminded Bryan.

"I know offense call fouls," Bryan said to Nate and then pointed at Kyle. "But why should I believe *his* call?"

Bryan's words stunned Kyle like a cold slap and left him speechless.

"What's *that* supposed to mean?" Nate asked.

Suddenly everything was dead quiet. Bryan glared at Kyle. The other boys froze. Kyle felt a drop of sweat trickle down his back. Kyle knew what was coming. He felt like he was falling and couldn't stop.

"Kyle, why don't you tell your friend about that great catch you made?" Bryan said with a phony smile smeared across his face.

Nate looked from Bryan to Kyle and back to Bryan. "What's going on?" he asked.

"You remember that great catch Kyle made in that game against us Cubs?" Bryan said to Nate. "Well, Jason Ridauer says Kyle didn't make the catch."

"Jason Ridauer is a jerk. What does he know?" Nate snapped back.

"Okay, so you don't believe Jason," Bryan said to Nate. "Go ahead, Kyle, tell him," Bryan sneered. "Did you make the catch or what?"

NINE

Kyle could feel his heart racing. "Why should I tell you anything, Bryan?" he blurted out. "You wouldn't believe me anyway." Then Kyle stormed off the court, grabbed his bike, and pedaled hard toward home.

"Kyle!" Nate called.

Bryan yelled after Kyle, "It doesn't matter! We're going to beat the Reds next Tuesday anyway."

How did I ever get myself into this mess? Kyle asked himself as he pedaled off into the streets. *That jerk Jason probably blabbed everything to everybody. All the Cubs must think I'm a cheater.*

Kyle struggled up the steep hill and had to pedal standing up. *Maybe I really should blow the Cubs game just to make it even.* Kyle finally came to the crest of the hill and began gliding down the other side, picking up speed with every second. *But the ump made the call. He said we won the game.* He gripped his brakes to slow down his bike. *And everybody thought I was a hero. Especially Dad and Coach Daye.*

At the bottom of the hill, he leaned into a left-hand turn. Suddenly a car horn honked. Kyle quickly swung right and almost lost control of his bike. The car sped by with its horn blaring.

Man, I won't solve my problems getting hit by a car. Kyle laughed nervously to himself. Then he looked both ways and safely turned toward home.

When Kyle got home, he walked into the kitchen and hung his helmet on a hook on the wall.

"Hey, champ," his father said from the kitchen table. "How's my star center fielder?"

"Okay, I guess," Kyle said, opening the refrigerator door. "There's nothing to eat around here."

"Hey, when's the big game against the Cubs?" Kyle's father smiled.

"Tuesday night."

"No way I'm going to miss that game. You ready?"

"I guess."

"Listen, Mom and Erin are at Erin's soccer game. Could you keep Honsey company while I run to the grocery store?"

"Sure, where is she?"

"In the den watching TV. How does grilled chicken sound for tonight?"

Kyle smiled and his stomach grumbled. "Great."

After Kyle's father left, the house was quiet. Kyle wandered into the den, still haunted by Bryan's stinging words.

Honsey had fallen asleep in an armchair. Her head of gray hair rested against the back of the easy chair. The hushed tones of a golf tournament on the television filled the room.

"Tiger needs the putt to stay tied for the lead," the announcer whispered as Tiger Woods approached the green.

Kyle tiptoed up to Honsey and carefully reached for the remote on the table beside her. Her eyes were closed and her breathing was low and steady.

Kyle aimed the remote at the screen. With a click, the golf tournament vanished and stock-car racing appeared.

"Hey. I was watching that!"

Kyle wheeled around. Honsey was wide awake.

"You scared me," Kyle said. "I thought you were asleep."

Honsey straightened herself in the chair. "I was just resting my eyes," she said.

Kyle clicked back to the golf tournament. Tiger Woods was squatting in back of his ball and studying the path to the hole.

"No wonder you fell asleep, Honsey. Golf is boring."

"Not to me."

"But nothing happens. Guys take twenty minutes to putt a ball ten feet," Kyle said as Tiger went to the other side of the hole and eyed his ball from that angle.

"It's the last game of real sportsman-ship," Honsey grumped.

54

"What?"

"It's the last game of real sportsman-ship," she repeated.

"What do you mean?" Kyle asked.

Honsey wagged a finger at the screen. "You don't see any umpires or referees out there. Golf is a game where the players call penalties on themselves."

"So they probably never call penalties at all," Kyle retorted as Tiger went back to his ball.

"Sure they do. In fact, Tom Kite, a famous golfer, was in a big tournament years ago. He had a small putt to make—a one-footer. He could have made it with his eyes shut. He was about to putt and saw his ball move a little—maybe his club accidentally tapped it. No one else saw it. But Kite counted it as an extra stroke on his scorecard. That's what you're supposed to do. It ended up costing him the trophy."

"No one else saw the ball move?" Kyle blurted out. "And he could have won the championship?"

Honsey nodded. "A gentleman is expected to tell the truth."

Kyle stared at the TV. Tiger Woods was gripping his club and carefully positioning himself for the shot. But Kyle wasn't really watching. He was thinking about the Reds, the Cubs, the "unbelievable" catch...and the truth.

The golf crowd roared as Tiger's putt glided along the shaved green grass and disappeared into the cup like a mouse into a mouse hole. Tiger pumped his fist. Honsey smiled.

"Okay, that's golf. Baseball is different," said Kyle. "You've got to have umpires in baseball."

"Maybe."

"Maybe?" Kyle asked, his head snapping up in surprise.

"Ever heard of Christy Mathewson?" Honsey asked.

Kyle thought for a moment. "Yeah, I think I saw his picture in one of your books about baseball," he said. He remembered a photo of an old-time ballplayer decked out in a short-brimmed cap and baggy flannel uniform. "He was a pitcher, right?"

Honsey nodded. "He won 373 games. My

father saw him pitch for the Giants. He said Mathewson was a real sportsman."

"What did he do?" Kyle laughed. "Call his own balls and strikes?"

"Almost." Honsey turned to Kyle. "You see, in the really early days of baseball, there was only one umpire for some games. If the umpire didn't see a close play on the bases and Christy Mathewson was pitching, the umpire would ask Christy Mathewson to make the call."

"Why?"

"Because everyone knew he was a gentleman. Everyone knew he was honest."

Kyle knew that Honsey knew everything there was to know about sports, but this story seemed hard to believe. "And Christy Mathewson would...make the call?" Kyle stammered. "Even against his own team? Even if it cost them a game?"

The camera zoomed in on Tiger as he walked to next hole, smiling and calmly waving to the fans.

"Yup. Even if it cost his team the game." Honsey sat back. "A gentleman is expected to tell the truth."

TEN

On Tuesday, Kyle sat on the Reds bench with his arms folded and his legs stretched out in front of him. He watched his teammates toss balls back and forth in the early evening light as they warmed up for the game against the Cubs in front of another big crowd.

Kyle's problem clung to him like the grass stains on his uniform. *Why did I ever fake that catch? It doesn't feel right to win the championship on a lie.... And Jason will tell everybody everything if we win.*

Kyle glanced over at the Cubs bench. Bryan Ford swung a weighted bat in the on-deck circle. The other Cubs paced restlessly. They were ready to play.

But Kyle wasn't. He looked over his shoulder at his whole family in the stands. His father smiled and pumped his fist. "Let's go, Reds!" he shouted to Kyle.

Kyle forced a smile and raised his fist toward his dad. "Yeah, let's go, Reds." Then he turned toward the field and took a deep breath. *I've gotta throw this game—even if Dad's here. Why didn't he just stay late at work today?*

"Come on in, Reds," Coach Daye called. Kyle got up slowly from the bench and joined his teammates in a circle. "All right, kids," Coach Daye said to the players. "We're ahead of the Cubs by one game. If we win tonight, we're the champions. If the Cubs win, our records will be tied and we'll have to have a playoff game. I don't want a playoff game with the Cubs. Let's win tonight!"

"Don't worry, Coach, we're gonna win tonight," Nate declared.

But Nate's brave talk wasn't much help. The Cubs jumped off to a quick lead in the first inning when Bryan Ford blasted a long drive over Claire's head in left field that drove in two runs.

The Cubs stretched their lead to 3–0 in the third inning when a ground-ball single to center hopped over Kyle's glove. Kyle didn't show much hustle, and the runner on first raced all the way home before Kyle got the ball back to the infield.

Alana, the Reds leadoff hitter in the bottom of the third, got on base, but strikeouts by Kyle and Salvador made it look like another no-run inning. Then a crucial double by Dylan sent Alana home and put the Reds back in the game. Adam struck out swinging and ended the inning.

The Cubs didn't score, so the Reds still were trailing 3–1 when Kyle ran off the field in the top of the fourth inning. He plopped down at the end of the bench, away from his teammates.

Nate and Claire wandered down the bench and sat beside Kyle. "Hey, what gives?" Nate asked straight off. "You sure don't act like you're playing for a championship. You sick or something?"

Kyle shook his head. "I don't know. I just can't get my head in the game."

"Can't get your head in the game?" Nate repeated. "This is for the championship!"

"Maybe it's better if we don't win," Kyle muttered.

"Are you nuts?"

Kyle stole a quick look down the bench and lowered his voice. "Everybody on the Cubs thinks I cheated."

"Who cares what they think?" Claire said. "Bryan and his buddies are a bunch of jerks. You said so yourself."

Kyle looked away.

Claire grabbed Kyle's arm. "Listen," she said, "maybe you don't care about winning, but the rest of us do." She pointed at Nate and the rest of the Reds lined up along the bench rooting for a comeback. "Stop thinking about that other game and start thinking about this one."

The Reds began to inch their way back in the bottom of the fourth inning. Tony and Max squeezed a single and a walk around a strikeout by Claire. Suddenly the Reds had runners on first and second, one out, and a glimmer of hope.

"Nate, Alana, and Kyle!" Coach Daye shouted. "Top of the order. Let's keep it going."

Nate sent a sweet line drive to center that grazed the outfielder's glove and kept going. Tony ran all the way home. Max advanced to second and Nate made it safely to first. The score was 3–2. The Reds badly needed a hit to push ahead.

Alana popped out for the second out. Now it was up to Kyle.

Runners on first and second, two outs, one run down. "Come on, Kyle!" Claire shouted from the bench. "Keep it going!"

Before Kyle stepped into the batter's box, he glanced back at his teammates. All the players were sitting on the edge of the bench, cheering their lungs out.

"Bring 'em around."

"Be a hitter. Be a hitter."

Kyle looked out at Ben Pickman, the Cubs pitcher.

"Two outs," Bryan Ford signaled from the back of the plate. "No batter."

The first pitch streaked toward the outside corner. Kyle stepped forward but hesitated. The umpire shot his right hand up in the air. "Strike one!" he bellowed.

Kyle held back on the next pitch too. But this pitch missed low.

One ball, one strike. Two outs, two on.

I hate holding back! Kyle said to himself. *It's like I'm not even playing!*

Ben threw the next pitch high. Bryan had to pop out of his catcher's crouch to grab it.

Two balls, one strike.

Kyle checked his swing on the next pitch as the ball sliced the heart of the plate.

"Strike two!"

"He's a looker!" Bryan shouted. "Throw strikes, Ben, baby. He couldn't hit a watermelon!"

Man, I hate losing to Bryan Ford! Kyle thought. He felt his whole body tense up, and he stepped out of the batter's box to cool down. He heard his father's voice above the crowd. "Swing level, Kyle. Only takes one."

I don't have to throw away the championship, Kyle told himself as he slowly stepped back into the batter's box. *I should just stick to my story. Nobody's going to believe Jason. He's such a lowlife.* Kyle glanced back at the Reds bench. *And everybody wants to win: my teammates, Coach Daye, Dad—and me!*

Kyle dug his foot into the back of the batter's box and peered out at the pitcher. The next pitch spun over the inside half of the plate. This time Kyle didn't hesitate. He uncoiled a smooth, hard swing.

Crack!

ELEVEN

The ball rocketed off Kyle's bat, and Kyle started to run. But the Cubs shortstop, Reed Johnson, took one step to his left and snagged the ball—and the Reds chances at tying the game.

Barely out of the batter's box, Kyle kicked the dirt and looked hopelessly at the sky. The Cubs almost danced off the field, shouting and still clinging to a 3–2 lead.

Kyle tossed his helmet back toward the bench and walked slowly to center field.

"Good rip. You were robbed," Claire said as she handed Kyle his glove. "That's swinging the bat like you mean it."

"We're still down a run," Kyle pointed out as the two friends jogged out to their places in the outfield.

"It's only the top of the fifth," Claire said. "We still have two more chances. You'll get up again."

The Reds kept it close in the top of the fifth. The Reds pitcher Adam Szwed whiffed two Cubs and Claire made a running catch to end the inning. No runs.

The Reds could not pull ahead in the bottom of the fifth. Salvador popped up for an out. Dylan and Adam got on base with one-out singles. Then Ben Pickman bore down and started firing fastballs. Tony popped up and Claire struck out swinging. No runs. The score was still 3–2.

Adam mowed down the Cubs batters—one, two, three—in the top of the sixth.

"Come on, Reds! Last ups!" Coach Daye yelled as the team ran in. "Max Singh leads off. Then the top of the order."

The Reds bench was bedlam. Kids were slapping each other on the back and clapping until their hands hurt.

"Come on, Max. Start us off."

"Look 'em over. We need base runners."

"Rally caps."

Kyle whipped his hat around and silently figured his chances for getting up to bat that inning. *Max, Nate, and Alana, and then me. Fourth up. Just need someone to get on base for me to get my ups.*

Max did not turn out to be that someone. The Reds sure-handed but light-hitting second sacker bounced out to first. One out.

Nate smacked a single into center field and gave Kyle and the Reds a chance. The bench was up and shouting.

"All right, Nate!"

"Clutch hit."

Coach Daye waved his score book above his head. "Alana is up. Kyle's on deck. Salvador is in the hole. Look 'em over. We need base runners!"

The Reds groaned as Alana lifted a lazy fly out to left. The Cubs left fielder made the easy catch and Nate had to dig back to first.

Two outs, runner on first. The Reds trailed 3–2 in the bottom of the last inning.

It was all up to Kyle.

"Come on, Kyle," his father called out. "Pick one you like and give it a ride."

Ben Pickman, the Cubs hurler, wiped the sweat from his brow and fired hard. Kyle swung nervously at the first pitch.

Strike one!

"He's a whiffer," Bryan taunted as Kyle stepped out of the box.

Just meet it, Kyle told himself.

The next pitch slipped just wide. Kyle kept the bat on his shoulder.

"Ball!" the umpire shouted.

Kyle let out a rush of air. *Whew!* he thought. *That was close.*

The Cubs pitcher wound up and snaked a fastball toward the outside corner of the plate. Kyle swung and drilled a line drive to right center field. The ball fell between two outfielders. Kyle roared around first and slid into second base. The Cubs safety fielder hustled the ball to home plate. Nate held up at third.

The Reds had runners at second and third. Two outs. They were still alive!

"Just need a single, Salvador," Kyle called as he popped up and brushed the dirt off his pants.

Coach Daye held two fingers above his head. "Two outs. Running hard on anything!" he shouted.

Crack!

Kyle's heart jumped when he heard the Reds cleanup hitter make contact with the ball. Kyle didn't wait to see where it was going. He took off for third base.

Nate dashed toward home and the Reds third-base coach gave Kyle the sign to keep moving. Nate scored and now the Reds championship dream rode with Kyle's flying feet. As Kyle rounded third, he could see Bryan with his catcher's mask thrown off, straddling home plate, waiting for the throw.

Kyle pumped his legs even faster, squeezing out every ounce of speed he had.

"Slide, Kyle, slide!" Nate shouted from the sidelines.

The ball bounced toward Bryan Ford just as Kyle dropped into his slide. Kyle's foot pushed up a storm of dirt as he stretched his leg toward the plate.

Bryan snagged the ball and swept his

glove across Kyle's leg. Kyle was moving so fast that his feet tangled with Bryan's and sent the Cubs catcher tumbling.

Dirt and dust were flying as Bryan struggled to his knees and frantically pushed his glove high in the air so the umpire could see he still had the ball. Kyle, breathing hard and fast, kept his eyes on the ump. He was hoping his foot had reached the plate before the tag.

The umpire looked from the ball, to the plate, to Kyle. And then he made his call.

TWELVE

Safe!" the umpire shouted as he spread his big arms wide above the two boys. Kyle fell back into the dirt in relief. The Reds had won the game, 4–3. They were the champions!

Bryan slumped back onto his legs and cried out, "Oh, come on, he was out!"

Within seconds, coaches and players were crowding around home plate. Mr. Rolfe, the Cubs coach, rushed up to the umpire. "No way he was safe!" he yelled. "My catcher was blocking the base. The runner never touched the plate!"

The umpire shook his head and yelled back, "The runner slipped under the tag, Coach! The tag was high."

Kyle's teammates pulled him up from the dirt and cheered wildly.

"What a play!"

"All right, Reds!"

"We're number one!"

Kyle brushed the dirt off his uniform, still a little dazed. He spotted his parents standing and cheering in the stands. It made him smile to see his father pumping his fist in the air. Honsey sat in her lawn chair, clapping her hands high above her head as loud as she could.

"Come on, champs," Mr. Daye called. "Let's line up and shake hands with the other team."

The two teams lined up and shook hands over home plate. The Reds grinned at each other and their fans. The Cubs were quiet, glancing up only long enough to whisper a half-hearted "good game" and offer a weak handshake.

Kyle, however, wasn't quite as happy as his teammates. As he moved from hand to hand, a knot tightened in his stomach. At first, Kyle had almost convinced himself that everything was okay. The Cubs had had their chance. The Reds had won this one fair and square. But as Kyle looked into the faces of the defeated Cubs, he thought about the other game—the one the Reds didn't win fair and square.

"Great game, kids!" Mr. Daye shouted above the celebrating players and parents. "I'll call everybody later about the trophies." He thrust his pointer finger in the air and sang out: "We're number one!"

The car ride home was like the one after the last game against the Cubs. Kyle's father talked about nothing but baseball. "What a game. What a game," he crowed. "When has a team ever won it all on a play at the plate like that?"

"The 1991 World Series, when the Twins beat the Braves 1–0 on a play at the plate," Honsey said.

Kyle's mother laughed. "Leave it to Honsey to know the answer to that one."

"And I was at the 1946 World Series when the Cardinals beat the Red Sox," Honsey said. "Enos Slaughter made his mad dash—all the way from first to home on a single."

"Was there ever a game you weren't at, Honsey?" Erin asked.

"I'm sure you're glad you were at this one," Kyle's father said.

Honsey nodded in agreement. "This is one of the best games I ever saw."

"It had it all," Kyle's dad said. "Good pitching, some spectacular plays in the field, a great comeback...and that play at the plate!" He tapped the steering wheel and laughed. "What a game!"

"Hey, when will you get your trophy?" Erin asked.

"Yeah," his father said. "I want to put it on the mantel."

"I don't know." Kyle shrugged. "Coach said he'd call us later." He stared out the window and wished silently that everyone would stop talking about the game. And that he could get the Cubs sad, beaten faces out of his mind.

Kyle's father kept chattering as he pulled the family van into the driveway. "And what about our star center fielder? He made a great catch to save a couple of runs, got a big hit to keep the rally going, and then turned on the jets to score the winning run!"

Kyle squirmed out of the backseat and bolted for the house.

"Is something wrong, Kyle?" his mother called after him.

"No," Kyle called back. "I…uh…just have to go the bathroom really bad."

"So what do you think, Honsey?" Kyle heard his father ask as he led Honsey up the walk. "Is your grandson going to be the next Willie Mays or the next Joe DiMaggio?"

Honsey stopped a moment and thought. "I think Ken Griffey Jr. might have been as good as either of them." Then she added, "But my grandson can play too."

Once inside, Kyle ran up to his room. He ripped off his uniform as quickly as he could and tossed it in a heap on the floor. *Maybe if I'm not in my uniform, Dad will stop talking about the game,* Kyle thought.

"Hey, here's the MVP," Kyle's father announced as Kyle came downstairs.

Rrrring! The telephone made Kyle jump.

"I've got it!" Erin called as she raced to the den.

"It's probably the papers again." Kyle's dad smiled.

"Kyle, it's for you!" Erin called. Kyle went to get it.

"Who is it?" he asked Erin nervously, remembering Jason's call from the previous week.

"It's Claire."

Kyle took the phone. "Hey, Claire. We're the champs!" he said, trying his best to sound cheerful.

"I'm not so sure." Claire's voice sounded down.

"What do you mean?"

"Coach Daye just called," Claire explained. "He said the Cubs are going to protest the game at the next league meeting."

"Protest the game? How can they protest the game?" Kyle demanded, his words tumbling out. "I was safe at home. The ump made the call."

"Not that game. The other game," Claire said.

"Which one?" The words almost got caught in Kyle's throat.

"You know, the one where you made that great catch over the fence."

Kyle fell silent.

"You made the catch, didn't you, Kyle?" Claire asked.

For a second, Kyle felt like blurting out the truth. But he couldn't tell anyone, not even Claire. He searched for a way to avoid the question. "I can't believe they're protesting the game!" he finally said.

"Yeah," said Claire. "Everyone knows you caught the ball."

Yeah, Kyle thought, *everybody but me.*

THIRTEEN

When Kyle and his father walked into the league meeting room, the warm, stale air almost pushed them back. "Boy, it's crowded in here," Kyle's father observed. "I'm glad your mom and Honsey decided not to come."

The twenty or so metal chairs on the room's small linoleum floor were already taken. More players and parents stood along the sides and back of the room, talking quietly and leaning against the walls.

The Reds and their families had gathered on one side of the room, and the Cubs on the other. A long table and three chairs—one for each of the league commissioners—sat in the front of the room. In front of the long table was a small podium for speakers who wanted to address the commissioners.

Kyle's mouth was suddenly dry and his heart beat hard against his chest. The hot air was hard to breathe. He felt like he was coming to bat with the bases loaded.

His heart almost stopped when he saw Jason Ridauer standing against the far wall next to Bryan Ford and some of the other Cubs. Jason shot him that same little crooked smile. Kyle looked away.

"There's Mr. Daye," Kyle said, spying his coach in the front row.

Mr. Daye stood and circled his arm and pointed to an empty chair next to him.

"Why don't you go sit with your coach?" Kyle's father suggested.

"Where will you be?" Kyle asked.

"I'll stand right back here. Go ahead."

Kyle threaded his way through the crowded room. He could feel the Cubs' eyes following him.

When Kyle got to the front of the room, Coach Daye patted the empty metal seat next to him. "Better sit close," he said. "The commissioners said that they might have to ask you a couple of questions."

"Ask me a couple of questions?" Kyle blurted out, his voice suddenly rising. "Why do they want to ask me questions?"

A door at the front of the room opened and the three commissioners walked in and sat at the front table. Mr. Kirsch, sitting in the middle chair, pounded a gavel against the table. The room fell quiet except for the slow ticking of the clock on the wall.

"All right, the meeting will come to order," Mr. Kirsch started. His voice was clear and strong. "We are here to consider a protest filed by the Cubs concerning this current season. Therefore, the commissioners ask Mr. William Rolfe, the coach of the Cubs, to come forward and state the reasons for the protest."

A low murmur rose as Mr. Rolfe stepped forward and stood at the small podium between the commissioners' table and the first row of chairs.

"The Cubs are protesting the Reds championship," he said, sounding to Kyle more like a lawyer on a TV show than a baseball coach. "We have reason to believe that Reds player Kyle Holt did not actually make a crucial catch in the second game between the Reds and the Cubs. But the ump said the catch was good, which resulted in the Cubs losing that game and, ultimately, the league championship."

Kyle suddenly felt sick to his stomach. Every inch of his body broke out in a cold sweat. He struggled to breathe the room's hot dry air.

Mr. Daye jumped to the podium. "This is ridiculous!" he shouted. "That game was played a week ago. They can't protest it now."

"We didn't know at the time that he didn't catch the ball!" Mr. Rolfe yelled above the rumble of voices and the sharp cracks of Mr. Kirsch's gavel.

"Everyone knows the umpire made the call!" Mr. Daye almost screamed. "He said Kyle caught the ball. The umps have to be able to make calls that stick. Just like the call at the plate in the last game!"

The whole room erupted with loud, sharp voices. Mr. Kirsch pounded his gavel, but could not silence the voices.

"The ump makes the call!"

"But what if he made the wrong call?"

"You guys are just sore losers!"

"Who's a sore loser?"

The voices around Kyle mixed with the voices in his head—the same voices that had been battling inside him ever since he had grabbed the ball out of the dirt in back of the outfield fence and held it over his head; the voices debating whether to tell the truth or to stick to his story and let everything blow over.

Then in an instant all the voices fell away and Kyle could only hear one voice inside his head. It was Honsey's voice. *A gentleman is expected to tell the truth.*

As if in a fog, Kyle found his way to the podium. The two coaches were still shouting at the commissioners and at each other. Mr. Kirsch stood and pounded his gavel. With the final crack of the gavel, the room, realizing that Kyle was standing at the podium, hushed.

Mr. Kirsch took a deep breath. "Is there something you want to say, Kyle?" he asked.

"Tell them you caught the ball, Kyle," Claire practically pleaded from the back wall.

I could tell them I caught the ball, Kyle thought. *I could stick to my story and no one would really know. No one would believe Jason.* For a second he almost convinced himself. Then he thought, *But I would know.*

Finally, Kyle found his own voice. "I didn't make that catch," he said softly.

"What did you say?" Mr. Kirsch asked, leaning forward.

Kyle spoke more loudly. "I said I didn't make that catch."

FOURTEEN

Everyone started talking at once. Mr. Rolfe and Mr. Daye tried to shout over the bedlam to the three commissioners. Mr. Kirsch pounded his gavel so hard that Kyle thought the table was going to split in two.

Kyle glanced around the room. The Cubs were celebrating. Bryan and Jason were trading high fives. On the other wall, the Reds slumped in stunned silence.

"Quiet." Mr. Kirsch kept pounding his gavel. "We need quiet, please."

The voices settled into a low murmur.

Mr. Kirsch pointed his gavel at the crowd. "We are going to let the two coaches speak," Mr. Kirsch said firmly. "And then the commissioners will make a decision about this." He looked to the commissioners seated to his left and right. They nodded.

"Mr. Rolfe." Mr. Kirsch pointed to the podium. "You're up."

"Well, I think it's pretty simple." The Cubs coach smiled. "It's clear that the umpires made the wrong call. Kyle Holt admitted tonight that he didn't make the catch."

Mr. Rolfe looked at Kyle, who was standing with Mr. Daye a step or two from the podium. "The commission should make the right call. They should declare that the Cubs won the second game. And declare that the Cubs are the league champions."

The Cubs players and parents burst into applause.

Mr. Kirsch pounded his gavel to quiet the crowd. "All right, Mr. Daye," he said. "It's your turn."

Mr. Daye stepped forward. "None of what has happened here tonight matters," he said through clenched teeth. "The teams agree before the game to play according to the umpires' calls. The umpires made the call." He jabbed his finger into the air. "They said Kyle made the catch. Their call should still stand."

Some of the Cubs parents protested in angry voices.

"That's crazy."

"Sit down."

"The Cubs are the real champs."

Coach Daye ignored them. "It's just like in the last game with the close play at the plate. The umps make the call. Both teams agreed to go by their decisions."

Kyle interrupted. "But this is different, coach," he insisted. "I *know* I didn't make the catch."

Coach Daye gave Kyle a stern look that said, *Keep quiet!*

The room filled again with shouts as the two teams tried to make their final points.

But Mr. Kirsch stood, held his hand up, and called for silence. "This is an unusual situation, to say the least," he said. "The commission will discuss the matter in private and make a decision."

"When?" someone asked from the back of the room.

"Tonight," Mr. Kirsch said curtly.

The three commissioners stood and filed into a small room in the front hall. The last one closed the door behind him.

A strange hush fell over the room after the commissioners left. The two groups stood apart in the uneasy quiet.

Coach Daye turned away from Kyle and joined the Reds and their parents. For the longest moment, Kyle stood alone in the front of the room, not sure of where to go. He certainly was not going to join the Cubs group, but he wasn't sure he was welcome in the Reds corner either. Finally, his father made his way to him. The two of them stood off to the side, near the Reds fans but not exactly with them.

"Kyle, I can't believe this," his father said, clearly pained. "You really didn't make that catch?"

Kyle slowly shook his head.

"What were you thinking, Kyle?"

"I just wanted us to win. I don't..." Kyle

couldn't finish his sentence. He shrugged and bit his lip.

"Oh, Kyle," his father sighed as he wrapped his arm around his shoulder. "We all love winning. But you know cheating isn't winning."

"I never should have faked that catch," Kyle said in a scratchy voice.

"Yeah," his father said. Then he pulled Kyle closer. "Look, I know it took a lot of guts to come here and tell the truth. You did the right thing tonight, Kyle."

"I don't think everybody else thinks I did the right thing tonight," Kyle said, his voice still shaky. When he looked around the room, he could see his teammates quickly looking away from him—even Claire. Nate was the only one who didn't turn away. He just shrugged.

"You did the right thing, Kyle. Know it," his father said. "I'm not very proud of Coach Daye right now. But I'm very proud of you for telling the truth tonight."

"Really?"

"Absolutely."

Kyle nodded. "Thanks." For the first time since he had faked the catch, Kyle felt like he could breathe again.

"What do you think they'll do, Dad?"

"The commissioners are good people. They'll be fair—"

Just then, the door to the commissioners' room swung open. The three men emerged unsmiling and stood behind their chairs at the wooden table. Mr. Kirsch rapped his gavel three times for silence. But the room was already quiet and the gavel sounded like thunder.

"The commission has come to a unanimous decision," Mr. Kirsch declared. Everyone in the room edged forward.

"We have decided that since the catch was not made, the Cubs are the winners of the game."

The Cubs whooped and hollered while Mr. Kirsch pounded his gavel.

"What about the championship?" Mr. Rolfe called. "Who are the champions?"

"This win gives the Cubs and the Reds identical records." Mr. Kirsch paused and took a quick breath. "The commission has ruled that the league championship will be decided by a single playoff game."

Again, voices filled the room.

"When?" someone called out.

Mr. Kirsch held up his hand for quiet. When the room settled, he said, "Monday night at 6 o'clock. Winners take all."

FIFTEEN

Monday evening was warm and clear, perfect weather for the battle between the Reds and Cubs.

All the Reds were warming up. Kyle, Nate, and Claire fired glove-popping throws back and forth to each other in the outfield. Pitcher Tom Kelly tested his fastball with Salvador, who crouched at the plate in his catcher's mask. The Cubs were doing leg stretches, head rolls, and jumping jacks on the sidelines.

"It seems like we've been playing these guys all year!" Kyle yelled out to Nate and Claire.

"Tonight's going to be great," Claire called in response.

"Think you can get your head in this game, Kyle?" Nate kidded.

"Oh, yeah, I'm ready," Kyle said.

Things were back to normal between Kyle and his two friends. At first Kyle wasn't sure if they ever would be. Claire didn't talk to Kyle for two days after the commissioners' meeting and Kyle felt like a jerk. He eventually went to Claire's house and apologized for letting her believe that Jason was the one who was lying. She said Kyle was lucky that the commissioner didn't make the Reds completely forfeit the championship.

Kyle knew she was right. If the commissioner hadn't okayed the playoff game, Kyle wouldn't have been able to face his teammates. It was funny, none of his other teammates mentioned the commissioners meeting—at least not to Kyle. They were pumped about the game and so was he.

Keeping his lie a secret had taken the fun out of the end of the season for Kyle. Now that the truth was out, everything felt different to him. The newly mowed grass seemed greener, the ball felt lighter, and the air seemed livelier with the sounds of baseball.

His mom and dad were really proud of him for telling the truth and Honsey was even prouder—she told him, "*Now* you're on your way to being another Christy Mathewson!" But the best part of all was that telling the truth had given Kyle back the game he loved to play—baseball.

"All right, bring it in, Reds!" Mr. Daye shouted, waving his score book over his head.

The Reds quickly crowded around their coach.

"I don't have to tell you that this one is for the big trophy," he told them. "I know you all want that trophy as much as I do. We always have close games against the Cubs, but let's beat them once and for all. No doubt about it." Mr. Daye paused and frowned at Kyle. "And no funny business tonight."

Kyle nodded, glancing at his teammates.

"Good," said Mr. Daye. "The Cubs are up first. So let's play ball."

Tom Kelly set the Cubs down in order in the top of the first. No runs, no hits, no errors.

Mr. Daye called out the batting order as the Reds raced in from the field. "Nate, Alana, and Kyle, let's start it off."

The Reds were up and cheering, pounding on the dugout fence as Nate approached the plate.

"Come on, Nate. Start us off."

"Look 'em over. Walk's as good as a hit."

"Just meet it, Nate. Just meet it."

The Cubs were ready. Taylor Hanley, the Cubs starting left-hander, was throwing hard. He struck out Nate swinging and got Alana out on a soft roller to second.

Kyle came to bat. There were two outs with nobody on base.

"Swing level, Kyle," his father called from his seat between Honsey and Kyle's mother. "Two-out rally!"

Kyle moved slowly from the on-deck circle toward the plate. He did not mind facing the fastballs of Taylor Hanley, but he was not looking forward to facing Bryan Ford.

Bryan stood behind home plate with his catcher's mask perched on his head. He watched Kyle approach the batter's box.

"You finally admitted that you didn't make the catch," Bryan said.

Kyle didn't say anything.

Bryan yanked down his mask and said, "We're still going to beat you guys."

"We'll see," Kyle said. Then he turned to the pitcher.

The first pitch was a fastball. Kyle cracked it up the middle, but Cubs shortstop Reed Johnson scooped it up and fired it to first.

The ball smacked into the first baseman's mitt a half-step before Kyle's foot came down on the bag. *Man, we're in a real ball game,* Kyle thought as he headed back to the bench for his glove.

The Reds and Cubs pitchers, Tom Kelly and Taylor Hanley, were locked in a tight duel. Tom Kelly was pitching a perfect game.

In the first four innings, not a single Cub reached base on a hit, walk, or even an error. And the Reds could only squeeze out a pair of singles.

"Come on, Tom!" Kyle yelled from center field as another Cub struck out in the top of the fifth. "Keep bringing the heat."

"Two outs," Kyle reminded Claire. He held up two fingers. "Good hitter coming up." Claire took two steps back.

Tom kept firing fastballs, but Reed Johnson kept fouling them off and worked the count to three balls and two strikes.

Kyle watched as Tom wound up for the payoff pitch. The ball darted along the outside edge of the plate as Reed Johnson held back.

Ball four! The umpire pointed to first base. The Cubs had their first base runner.

Kyle punched a fist into his glove and then waved Claire back a couple more steps. "Bryan's coming up," he called to her. "Better play him deep and make sure nothing gets in back of us."

"Throw strikes, Tom!" Claire yelled.

The first fastball skipped in the dirt in front of home plate. Salvador Rodriguez, the Reds catcher, blocked the ball, but Reed took off for second.

Kyle raced in to back up the throw to second base. Sure enough, Salvador's throw bounced past second, but Kyle was there to pounce on the ball before the runner could move up to third.

"Good hustle," Claire called as Kyle jogged back—way back—to deep center field.

Kyle nodded, but he knew that the Reds and Cubs were caught in a close one. This was the kind of game where one play, one pitch, one mistake could mean the difference between winning and losing.

"Come on, Tom!" he yelled. "Keep bringing the heat."

Kyle winced as the second pitch to Bryan Ford flew wide.

Two balls, no strikes to Bryan, he thought. *That's trouble.*

"Come on, Tom. He's just looking."

Bryan was not just looking on the next pitch. He swung hard and drove the ball deep to left center field.

Kyle raced to the fence, his mind flashing back to another high fly off Bryan Ford's bat. But this time, there was no leap, no great catch, no chance.

The ball easily cleared the fence and disappeared into the trees. It was gone.

SIXTEEN

Rally caps!" Kyle shouted as he raced into the Reds dugout. Kyle tossed his glove onto the Reds bench and turned his hat around. He cheered along with his teammates.

Coach Daye waved his hands above his head. "Over here, everybody. Listen up."

The Reds gathered around their coach.

"We're only down by two runs and we have two more times at bat to come back," he said in a calm voice. "We need base runners, so look the pitches over. Don't swing at any bad pitches. Maybe we can get some walks."

"And watch me for the bunt signal." Coach Daye demonstrated with a sweep of his hand across his cap brim and a tap to his left arm. "We may put on a play."

He clapped his hands, glanced at the score sheet, and announced, "Dylan, Adam, Tony, and then Claire. Let's get some runners on."

The Reds rally caps didn't bring luck right away. Dylan slapped a comebacker straight to the Cubs pitcher for the first out.

Kyle pressed against the dugout fence as Adam prepared to bat.

"Come on, Adam. Start us off. Look 'em over. Walk's as good as a hit."

Adam Szwed dug into the batter's box and battled Taylor, the Cubs pitcher, on every pitch. He fouled off several pitches until the count was full.

The Reds bench was up and screaming.

"Good sticker!"

"Come on, Adam. Hang in there."

"Make it good."

Taylor Hanley's final pitch flew high and Adam dropped his bat and trotted to first. The Reds had a runner on!

"Come on, Tony," the Reds called. "Keep it going!"

Tony Skladany rested one foot out of the batter's box and looked at Coach Daye. The Reds coach swept his hand across the brim of his cap and down his left arm.

Kyle elbowed Nate. "Coach is putting on the bunt sign."

The two friends leaned forward as Tony squared around and bunted. The ball plunked off the bat and rolled lazily along the third-base line. The Cubs stood by helpless as the ball settled at their feet just inside the foul line.

The Reds had runners at first and second with Claire coming to bat.

Claire battled just as hard as Adam had. She fouled off fastball after fastball and finally popped one just past the Cubs second baseman.

The Reds runners were off. Adam rounded third and raced across home plate for the run! The Cubs right fielder snared the ball and fired a one-hop strike to third base to nab the sprinting Tony.

"You're out!" the umpire signaled as the Cubs third baseman slapped the tag on the sliding Reds runner.

Kyle stood by the bench and threw his hands in the air. "Oh, no way!" he protested.

"I hate to say it, but I think he had him," Nate said.

Max struck out swinging, and Kyle and the rest of the Reds raced out to their positions. They were trailing 2–1.

After a quick one-two-three inning, the Reds raced back to their bench, still down by only a run. The team jumped around the bench, unable to hold in their excitement. It was the bottom of the last inning. If the Reds could pull ahead, they would be the champs!

Nate, Alana, and Kyle, the first three Reds batters, stood near the on-deck circle.

"Taylor's getting tired," Kyle observed, motioning toward the pitcher's mound.

"Yeah," Alana agreed. "He isn't popping the catcher's glove like he did in the first inning."

Kyle smiled at his teammates. "Let's get him," he said.

Sure enough, Nate jumped on the first fastball and lashed a hard single to left. Alana followed with a lucky looper that fell in front of the Cubs left fielder.

Kyle stepped to the plate with a pair of Reds runners on the base path and nobody out.

Both benches and the fans in the stands were on their feet and clapping. Kyle was almost shaking with excitement. He was pumped and ready to swing.

But when he looked down the third-base line, he saw Coach Daye sweep his hand across his cap and tap his left arm.

Oh, no, not the bunt signal, Kyle thought. *I want to knock one out of the park.* For a moment, Kyle thought about pretending to miss the bunt signal and swinging away. But he changed his mind. *I'm not faking anything anymore,* he thought.

Kyle plopped a perfect sacrifice bunt to the Cubs third baseman, making the first out, but moving the Reds runners to second and third.

Coach Daye and the Reds were on their feet when Kyle returned to the bench. They shook his hand and patted his back for a job well done.

Kyle stood at the dugout fence and smiled. For the first time since the meeting with the league commissioners, Kyle felt like he was really part of the team again.

"Come on, Salvador!" he shouted. "Knock 'em in."

The tired Cubs pitcher wound up and threw. The ball sped toward the heart of the plate, and Salvador was ready. Swinging level, he sent the ball high into left center field.

Every eye in the park followed the flight of the ball. Kyle pressed against the fence. Nate and Alana, the Reds runners, stood halfway between the bases, almost frozen in place, waiting to see what would happen.

The Cubs center fielder leaped, stretching and straining for the ball. He tumbled over onto the grass. But Kyle saw the ball bouncing happily to the fence.

It was a hit! The runners were off. Nate crossed home plate with the tying run. Alana was right behind him. As she jumped on home plate, she was swept up in a flood of Reds players streaming out of the dugout.

The Reds had won 3–2. They were really the champs!

The teams lined up to shake hands.

"Good game, Bryan," Kyle said when he finally reached the Cubs catcher.

"Good game, Kyle," Bryan said matter-of-factly. "We'll beat you guys next time."

"We'll see," Kyle replied.

Just then Kyle spotted Jason watching him from the Cubs dugout. This time Kyle didn't care. He just turned and looked for his family. And there they were, walking toward him. Kyle ran to them. "What a great game!" he yelled.

"I'll say!" his father shouted. "How often does a team win the pennant in a one-game, winners-take-all playoff?"

"Well, the Yankees beat the Red Sox in a one-game playoff in 1978," Honsey said before anyone had taken a breath. "And then there were the Indians in 1948—"

"Don't tell me you were at those games too, Honsey!" Kyle laughed.

"No." Honsey smiled. "But your grandfather and I were in the Polo Grounds when Bobby Thomson hit his home run in 1951 the day the Giants beat the Dodgers in a playoff."

"Honsey, you know everything," Kyle laughed. And, thinking back to all her stories about sports and golf and about Christy Mathewson, Kyle believed she did.

THE END

CHRISTY MATHEWSON THE REAL STORY

Christy "Matty" Mathewson was a great pitcher who played major league ball for seventeen years—from 1900 to 1916. Any baseball record book will tell you that he was one of five players in the first group that was ever admitted to the Baseball Hall of Fame.

Mr. Mathewson, who was called Big Six, stood six feet one and a half inches tall at a time when most players were much shorter. He won 373 games and lost only 188. He also had an amazing 2.13 earned-run average. That means that the other team only earned (scored) about two runs a game—not counting runs scored because someone on Mr.

Hall of Fame pitcher Christy Mathewson played major league baseball from 1900 to 1916.

Mathewson's team made an error. Mr. Mathewson also pitched eighty shutouts (games in which the other team didn't score at all).

What the record books don't tell you is that Mr. Mathewson was as famous for being a great sportsman as he was for being a great pitcher.

In the early 1900s, baseball was a rough, dirty sport. Players would break the rules if they thought it would help their team win. Fielders occasionally tripped base runners and grabbed them by the belt to slow them down. Players sometimes stomped on their opponents' feet with their spiked shoes. Hall of Famer Ty Cobb would even sharpen his spikes before games. Fights among players, fans, and even umpires were common.

Christy Mathewson became a new kind of baseball hero. As Honsey said in *Winners Take All,* he was a gentleman.

Mr. Mathewson didn't yell at the umpires, mope around when calls went against him, or quit when he was playing badly or his team was losing by a landslide. He loved winning, but when he lost he held his head high and praised the other team for a game well played. As one reporter said: "In victory he was admirable, but in defeat he was magnificent."

He was so honest that after a controversial game during the hard-fought 1908 pennant race, Mr. Mathewson told league officials that his teammate, Fred Merkle, had not touched second base during a crucial play. Mr. Mathewson's honesty cost the Giants the game and forced a one-game playoff with the Cubs that the Giants lost. Being honest was more important to Mr. Mathewson than a pennant or even a chance at the World Series.

Mr. Mathewson was college educated at a time when most ballplayers did not even go to high school. He was an A student who starred in football, basketball, and baseball at Bucknell University in Pennsylvania. Mr. Mathewson even helped write one of the first and best baseball books: *Pitching in a Pinch.*

Being a gentleman did not mean that he did not want to win. Christy Mathewson was a fierce competitor. But he didn't just like to win at baseball. He competed intensely in every game he played. He was an ace at cards as well as a champion checkers player who could play several opponents at the same time.

But Mr. Mathewson was best at baseball. The fabulous memory that made him so good at cards and checkers helped him on the mound. Mr. Mathewson could remember every pitch from every game. If a batter hit a certain pitch hard, Mr. Mathewson would be sure not to serve up that same pitch to that batter again. Armed with pinpoint control and his famous "fadeaway" pitch (which broke in the opposite direction of most curveballs), Mr. Mathewson piled up innings and wins for the Giants.

Mr. Mathewson was at his best in the big games. In the 1905 World Series, he had the most amazing Fall Classic ever for a pitcher. Mr. Mathewson started three games against the American League champions, the Philadelphia Athletics. Three games. Three wins. Three complete game shutouts. That's right, Christy Mathewson pitched twenty-seven innings against the best team in the American League and did not surrender a single run. The Giants won the Series four games to one.

So Christy Mathewson knew something about winning. But he also knew what Kyle had to learn the hard way. Mr. Mathewson knew that the only real win is when you win fair and square.

* * *

Honsey was also right about golfer Tom Kite. When he was playing in the 1978 Colgate Hall of Fame Classic in Pinehurst, North Carolina, he faced a small putt on the fifth green in the final round. He was just a couple of strokes behind Tom Watson, who was in the lead. Just before Mr. Kite was about to knock his ball into the hole, he saw it move. Nobody else did. According to the rules, a golfer gets a penalty of one stroke if the ball moves—even a little—while the golfer is lined up to hit it. So when Mr. Kite's scorekeeper was about to mark down four strokes for the hole, Mr. Kite told him to mark down five. He finished the tournament one stroke behind Mr. Watson!

He didn't get the trophy that year, but the following year Mr. Kite was recipient of the Bob Jones Award—the United States Golf Association's highest award presented for outstanding sportsmanship.

Tom Kite is not the only good sport in golf. Justin Leonard had the same thing happen to him in the Kemper Open in June 2000. Leonard played by the rules and counted the extra stroke.

The stroke did not cost Justin Leonard the tournament—he finished two strokes behind the winner—but it did cost him about $144,000 in prize money.

Acknowledgments

Scot Mondore—ace researcher at the Baseball Hall of Fame—came through for me once again with a lot of great information, this time about Christy Mathewson. I also got help from author Ray Robinson and his book *Matty, An American Hero*. Eddie Frierson, president of the Mathewson Foundation and an author/actor who performs a one-man show based on Christy Mathewson's life, helped me out too.

When I had trouble ferreting out the facts about golfer Tom Kite's calling a penalty on himself, I called Rand Jerris, Ph.D., librarian at the USGA (United States Golf Association). He got back to me with amazing speed and accuracy.

ABOUT THE AUTHOR

One of Fred Bowen's earliest memories is watching the 1957 World Series with his brothers and father on the family's black-and-white television set in Marblehead, Massachusetts. Mr. Bowen was four years old.

When he was six, he was the batboy for his older brother Rich's Little League team. At age nine, he played on a team, spending a lot of time keeping the bench warm. By age eleven, he was a Little League All Star.

Mr. Bowen has also coached more than a dozen kids' basketball teams.

His dog is named Matty—after the gentleman pitcher Christy "Matty" Mathewson.

Mr. Bowen is the author of a number of sports novels for young readers. He lives in Silver Spring, Maryland with his wife Peggy Jackson. His daughter is a college student and his son is a college baseball coach.

Mr. Bowen writes a sports column for kids in the *Washington Post*.

Be sure to check out the author's websites.
www.fredbowen.com
www.SportsStorySeries.com

Become a fan of Fred Bowen on Facebook!

HEY, SPORTS FANS!

Don't miss these action-packed books by Fred Bowen...

Want more?

All-Star Sports Story Series

T. J.'s Secret Pitch
PB: $5.95 / 978-1-56145-504-1 / 1-56145-504-0

T. J.'s pitches just don't pack the power to strike out the batters, but the story of 1940s baseball hero Rip Sewell and his legendary eephus pitch may help him find a solution.

The Golden Glove
PB: $5.95 / 978-1-56145-505-8 / 1-56145-505-9

Without his lucky glove, Jamie doesn't believe in his ability to lead his baseball team to victory. How will he learn that faith in oneself is the most important equipment for any game?

The Kid Coach
PB: $5.95 / 978-1-56145-506-5 / 1-56145-506-7

Scott and his teammates can't find an adult to coach their team, so they must find a leader among themselves.

Playoff Dreams
PB: $5.95 / 978-1-56145-507-2 / 1-56145-507-5

Brendan is one of the best players in the league, but no matter how hard he tries, he can't make his team win.

Winners Take All
PB: $5.95 / 978-1-56145-512-6 / 1-56145-512-1

Kyle makes a poor decision to cheat in a big game. Someone discovers the truth and threatens to reveal it. What can Kyle do now?